Ladybird

This Little Story
belongs to

PRISCA

A catalogue record for this book is available
from the British Library

Published by Ladybird Books Ltd
A subsidiary of the Penguin Group
A Pearson Company
© LADYBIRD BOOKS LTD MCMXCVII

LADYBIRD and the device of a Ladybird are trademarks of
Ladybird Books Ltd Loughborough Leicestershire UK

Big
Little
Bus

by Nicola Baxter
illustrated by Toni Goffe

"BOOP! BOOP! Move over, Little Bus," boomed the Big Bus, rumbling out of the garage.

"Oooh nooo," tooted the Little Bus, "I've got to go! There'll be lots of passengers for the Grand Pet Show!"

"Lots!" laughed the Big Bus. "But you're so LITTLE! You can't carry *lots* of anything!"

The Little Bus chugged off down the road, feeling smaller than ever.

At the first bus stop, a *very* tired lady was waiting. But she was not alone. She had a baby in a buggy, and a puppy (called Pickle), and six *enormous* bags of shopping.

"Is there room for us?" she called.

"Well…," sighed the Little Bus. "I'm not a very *big* bus. But I'll try."

So the lady with the baby climbed on board.

"I *do* feel better with passengers inside!" thought the Little Bus.

But as she trundled along…

…the puppy started to wriggle

…the shopping bags started to jiggle

…and the baby started to cry.

Soon there were bottles and tins
and baby things all *over* the bus.

What a TERRIBLE mess!

At the next stop was a man in a suit.

"Can I get a seat with my parrot called Pete?" he asked.

The Little Bus sighed. "I'm quite full already, but climb up and see!"

I feel wobbly on my wheels!

So the man got on the bus. He picked up the bottles and tins and baby things. He smiled at the lady and made faces at the baby.

The parrot called Pete hopped up on the seat. Pete wiggled, the baby giggled and Pickle sat still at last.

At the next stop, there were two more passengers.

"Can you squeeze us in?" called a lady in a hat with a very fat cat.

"I'm not very big," called the Little Bus, "but there's room for two!"

The lady in the hat bustled to the back. The man in a suit tried to pat the fat cat.

"Puss Puss Purrfect is rather shy," said her owner, with a sigh.

On went the Little Bus. The baby went to sleep. Sssh! And the parrot called Pete found something to eat.

At the next bus stop, three little girls stood in a row.

They called, "Can you take us to the Grand Pet Show?"

"Yes! Jump on board... all of you!" said the Little Bus.

For each little girl had two white mice, who scampered and skipped and twizzled their tails.

At the next bus stop there was one small boy.

"Is there room for me?" he called.

"Well…," said the Little Bus.

But the lady in the hat called out, "What's in that box? Will it upset Puss Puss Purrfect?"

And the little girls cried, "Does it eat pets that scamper and skip?"

And everyone else whispered, "*Ssshhhhh!* Will it wake the baby?"

And they all got off the bus to have a look.

The little boy held his box proudly. "In here," he said, "are exactly one hundred and twenty-four crawly caterpillars. They're *very* quiet and they *cannot* escape!"

"My baby is very crawly and he *often* tries to escape!" said the lady.

But the box *was* tied up well, and the little boy got on the bus.

So the lady with the baby and the buggy and the puppy (called Pickle)...

the man in a suit with a parrot (called Pete)...

the lady in a hat with a very fat cat...

the three little girls with their six white mice...

and the boy with a box of one hundred and twenty-four crawly caterpillars...

and the Little Bus set off...

for the Grand Pet Show.

But when they arrived, the Big Bus was already there.

"BOOP! BOOP!" he boomed. "I've brought sixty-six passengers all the way here."

"Only *sixty-six*?" tooted the Little Bus. "*I've* done better than that! But I'm not very good at counting."

Oh no, not him again!

"I am! I counted *all* my caterpillars.
Now…" said the little boy,

"The lady and her baby make one and two… and the puppy (called Pickle) makes three.

Four and five are the man in a suit and his parrot (called Pete)…

the lady in the hat and her very fat cat make six and seven… *but* the cat isn't fat! She's had four kittens! Eight, nine, ten, eleven!

The three little girls and their six white mice add up to… twenty!

I'm twenty-one," said the boy, undoing his box, "and here are exactly one hundred and twenty-four...

beautiful BUTTERFLIES!"

The passengers cheered and the baby chuckled.

The puppy barked and the parrot squawked.

And while the butterflies fluttered high overhead, everyone waved goodbye and said,

"You're the

BIGGEST

Little Bus in the world!"